Wings of Icarus

Jenny Oldfield
Illustrated by Bee Willey

A & C Black • London

White Wolves Series Consultant: Sue Ellis,
Centre for Literacy in Primary Education

This book can be used in the White Wolves Guided Reading
programme with more experienced readers at Year 3 level.

First published 2007 by
A & C Black
Bloomsbury Publishing Plc
50 Bedford Square
London
WC1B 3DP

www.acblack.com

ISBN 978-0-7136-8419-3

A CIP catalogue for this book is available from the British Library.

Printed and bound by CPI Group (UK) Ltd, Croydon, CR0 4YY

5 7 9 10 8 6 4

Contents

Chapter One   5

Chapter Two   14

Chapter Three   20

Chapter Four   28

Chapter Five   37

About the Author   45

Chapter One

"Icarus, son, come here. I have something to show you," Daedalus called.

The boy stood on the shore and stared out at the sparkling Aegean Sea. "What lies beyond the water?" he wondered.

"Icarus!" his father called again.

At last, Icarus turned.

Daedalus held a large shell, which he was eager to show him. "Come!" he cried.

Icarus ran to join his father.

"Look into this shell," Daedalus urged. "Feel how smooth it is."

The boy touched the inside of the shell with his fingertips. He loved the bright pink surface, smooth and shiny as polished marble.

"Now hold it to your ear," his father said. "What do you hear?"

Icarus listened. The shell sent
forth a soft whoosh of sound, like
distant waves
breaking on
the shore.
"I hear the
ocean,"
he replied.

Daedalus
nodded. "This
shell is a wonderful thing.
It contains the song of the sea."

Icarus smiled. "Let us take it
home so that I can always hear
the waves, first thing in the
morning and last thing at night."

Daedalus knew why his son said this. "And you can dream of the Aegean Sea and what lies beyond," he murmured with a sad smile. "You will picture an escape from this island, which is our prison."

Icarus carried the shell with
him. "Yes, I will dream," he
agreed. "And one day, perhaps,
my dream will come true."

That night, Icarus lay with the
shell beside him on his pillow.
But he did not dream of the sea.
Instead, a monster broke out from
the boy's sleeping world and
breathed over
him. It had the
body of a
man but
the ugly
head of a bull.

"Father, it is the Minotaur!"
Icarus cried out.

Daedalus
gathered his
white robes
around him
and came
running
with a
flame to
light the dark room. "There
is nothing here," he said softly.

But Icarus shook with fear.
"The monster was here. I saw his
sharp horns, I felt his hot breath
upon me!"

Daedalus sat with his son until
the nightmare faded. His thoughts
were dark because it was he who
had created the bull-monster
and brought him to life for the
amusement of the king's wife,
Pasiphae.

But the Minotaur, once alive, would not be tamed and King Minos had grown angry with Daedalus.

And now, though Daedalus had trapped the greedy monster in the centre of a great maze and bravely slain him, the king would not forgive its inventor.

 "Daedalus, from henceforth you will live as a prisoner on the island of Crete!" he had declared. "I will exile you there, where you built the maze, forever!"

Forever! The word echoed around the walls of Icarus's room. The torch flame died and Daedalus sat in darkness. "It is my fault that my son is lonely," he thought. "He is banished with me and, though he loves me, he wishes to live in the world with other boys and girls."

Troubled, Daedalus sat until dawn, wondering in vain how he could give his son the gift of freedom.

Chapter Two

The next day, Icarus quickly
forgot his nightmare and went as
usual to explore the seashore. He
climbed high rocks and gazed at
the empty horizon. He swam in

clear pools and dived deep below
the surface.

He was away for hours, until
Daedalus grew concerned and
went looking for him. He soon
found Icarus swimming in the
open sea, his head bobbing
between the white-capped waves.

Daedalus cupped his hands
around his mouth. "Swim to the
shore!" he bellowed. "The current
will carry you out to sea!"

Icarus heard the warning and felt the tug of the water. He was far from the shore, so he kicked hard and fought the current, arriving at last on dry land.

"Foolish boy," Daedalus complained.

Icarus waded from the water, shaking salty drops from his hair. "See, I am a good swimmer," he replied proudly. "I am young and strong."

Daedalus wanted to say more but he bit his tongue. He saw that in one breath his son was a boy afraid of bad dreams, but in the next he was proud and reckless, an almost-man.

"I am hungry!" Icarus declared, striding towards home.

"I have invented great wonders out of wood and stone," Daedalus said to himself, as he walked among olive trees on a lonely hill. "In the whole of Athens there was no inventor clever enough to rival me."

Birds flew in from the sea and settled in the low trees. The sun sank slowly in the west.

"Yet for all my skills I cannot find a way to escape this island," he muttered.

With his head bowed and his gaze fixed on stony ground, he walked slowly into the sunset.

"I love my father with all my heart," Icarus thought. "I love this island, which is warm and sunny, and full of beautiful things."

He paused by the shore and looked back at the dark maze with the tower at its centre, where white birds roosted.

"But it is not enough!" he said, striding on angrily as the red sun sank into the sea.

Chapter Three

"King Minos is lord of earth and sea," Daedalus explained over supper that night. "For as long as he lives, we are condemned to exile here."

"But how can it be that the king, great as he is, rules the wide sea?" Icarus demanded. "Surely we could leave here in search of another island, where there are people who would be our friends."

"My son, you are hasty,"
Daedalus frowned. "The waves
are strong. You know how easily
a swimmer may drown."

"Then we must build a boat
that will carry us across the
waves," came the swift reply.

Daedalus stared into the embers of the glowing fire. "Who will row the boat?" he muttered, knowing that he had grown old and weak.

"I will, Father! And we will take bread and meat for our long journey."

The boy was so excited and went to bed so full of hope that Daedalus could not bear to deny him. So he sat with parchment and quill through the long night, and by the light of a candle he drew plans for a boat, which they might build together.

In the morning, he showed them to his son.

"We will use only the stoutest timbers!" Icarus declared. He helped Daedalus fashion beams and long planks of wood, working from dawn until dusk.

Daedalus consulted his plans. "This beam must be longer and more curved," he said. "We must

take out the iron nails from the
roof of our house. Then we will use
them to secure the planks to the
framework of the boat."

For many hot days, father
and son worked on the seashore
to finish their vessel.

But still Daedalus was uneasy.
"Icarus is only a boy. His arms
are weak. How can he row over

that distant horizon?" he asked himself.

He puzzled over his plans until he found an answer.

Then he unrolled his parchment for his son to see.

"Icarus, I have invented a way for the wind to carry us across the waves."

"The wind?" Icarus echoed. "How can that be?"

"See here." Daedalus pointed to his drawing. "We must fix a tall pole in the centre of our boat and tie to it a large square of strong cloth. When the wind blows, the cloth will billow and the force of it will speed us across the water."

Icarus nodded. He believed in his father's clever plan, though it had never been tried before.

So they worked for two more days to erect the pole and sew the sail. Then father and son dragged their boat to the water's edge.

Chapter Four

The wind blew from the north as Daedalus and Icarus stepped into the boat.

"Unfurl the sail," Daedalus said, steadying himself at the rudder.

Icarus untied the strings and let the sail flap. The wind caught it; the boat jolted forward from the shore.

"It works!" Icarus gasped.

"Yes, it works," Daedalus echoed, tugging the rudder to steer the boat clear of some sharp rocks.

His son gazed ahead at the wide blue sea. He felt the wind in his hair, the sun on his face and a salty spray from the waves.

But then the sky suddenly grew dark and the wind strengthened. The waves lashed against the boat and tugged at their precious sail until it tore apart, leaving them at the mercy of the angry sea.

"Hold tight to me!" Daedalus
cried above the roar of the waves.

Icarus held on through the
wind and rain. In the morning, the
sun rose and showed them that
they were back where they had
started – on the craggy shore of
their prison isle.

"King Minos sent the storm to show us that he is lord of the sea," Daedalus said.

Icarus didn't answer. His eyes were dull. Since the day of the storm he had put aside his shell and no longer listened to the song of the sea.

"Lord of the sea and of the earth," Daedalus admitted. Then he studied his parchments for many days, looking for a new answer that would restore hope to his son's despairing eyes.

"But not lord of the sky!" he said at last. He strode from the house and looked up. He saw the big white gulls sail on warm currents of air, then rest on the battlements of the tower.
"I am certain that King Minos does not rule the heavens!" he cried.

"We will make wings and fly away," Daedalus told Icarus. "We will soar through the heavens like birds and land where we please."

Once more, the boy eagerly accepted his father's plan.

"Bring me small feathers so that I can make wings as strong and light as those of a swan," Daedalus said.

So Icarus ran off and collected small, down-soft feathers, which his father glued to a light, wooden frame, using soft wax to secure them.

"The wax will cool and harden," Daedalus said. "But now you must fetch me large feathers to make the wings strong."

Icarus was tired, but he set off once more.

Soon, he returned with an armful of long, straight feathers, which he dropped at his father's feet. "Is this enough?" he asked.

"Almost, my son," Daedalus replied.

But a sudden wind came and scattered the feathers, so Icarus had to run after them and gather them again, and the sun had set by the time he returned.

Then his father took pity on him. "Sleep now," he said.

So Icarus laid his head of dark curls on a pillow of soft feathers. And, as he slept, he dreamed of the sun.

Chapter Five

Daedalus worked as Icarus slept. By morning, he had finished the wings and he went with his son through the dark maze to the tower at its centre.

"We will climb to the top and watch how birds fly," he said. "We will learn how they beat their wings to catch the currents of air."

Icarus could hardly wait.

He ran ahead to the top of
the tower and looked out to sea.
Around his head, white birds
soared. "Soon," he promised
himself. "Soon I will be free!"

Then Daedalus came and strapped the wings to his son's back. "Take care not to dip too low towards the sea," he warned. "If your wings get wet, they will not carry you back up to the sky."

Icarus nodded. "Be quick, Father," he pleaded, as Daedalus buckled the straps.

"But do not fly too high," his father cautioned. "If you fly too close to the sun, it will melt the wax, and the feathers will fall from the frame."

"Please hurry!" Icarus begged. As he spread his arms wide and the wind caught his wings, he heard the call of lands beyond the sea.

Meanwhile, Daedalus struggled to attach his own wings. "Wait until I am ready," he told his son. "We will fly together."

But Icarus already felt the power of the wind. He beat his wings and rose from the tower.

His father looked up in fear.
"Take care, Icarus!"

Icarus did not answer. He beat
his wings again and soared into
the air, joining the birds of the sky.

Daedalus watched, helpless, as
Icarus rose higher towards the sun.
"Come back!" he cried.

But Icarus flew on, closer still
to the burning orb. He felt its
golden glow and was dazzled
by its brilliant light.

"I am free!" he sighed.

From the dark tower, Daedalus
saw his son falter in his flight.

He saw the sun melt the wax and the white feathers fall. They spiralled through the air towards the sea.

And then Icarus could fly no more. He plummeted down, beating his arms in vain.

The beautiful boy fell into
the sparkling Aegean Sea,
and drowned.

"Oh, Icarus,
my son!"
Daedalus
whispered,
as he felt his
heart break in two.

Afterwards, Daedalus named the
spot where his son fell the Sea of
Icarus and, though it happened
long ago, you may sail in those
waters to this very day.

About the Author

Jenny Oldfield was born in Yorkshire, where she still lives with her two daughters, Kate and Eve. She read English at university and then pursued a number of jobs before she started writing at the age of 24. She has now published over 50 books for adults and children, many in popular series including *My Magical Pony* and *Definitely Daisy*. Jenny has always loved the outdoors and when she isn't writing, she loves horse riding, playing tennis, walking and travelling to far-off places.

Other White Wolves Myths and Legends...

PANDORA'S BOX

Rose Impey

When the world was new, Prometheus
made Man out of clay and gave him life.
But then he stole fire from the gods and
made Zeus angry. The Top God was
determined to have his revenge and
make Man suffer. So he gave him
Woman, who was perfect in every
way, except one . . .

Pandora's Box is a modern retelling
of the classic Greek myth.

ISBN: 9 780 7136 8420 9 £4.99